The Magic Secrets Box

The Enchanted Forest Mystery

SUE MONGREDIEN

stripes

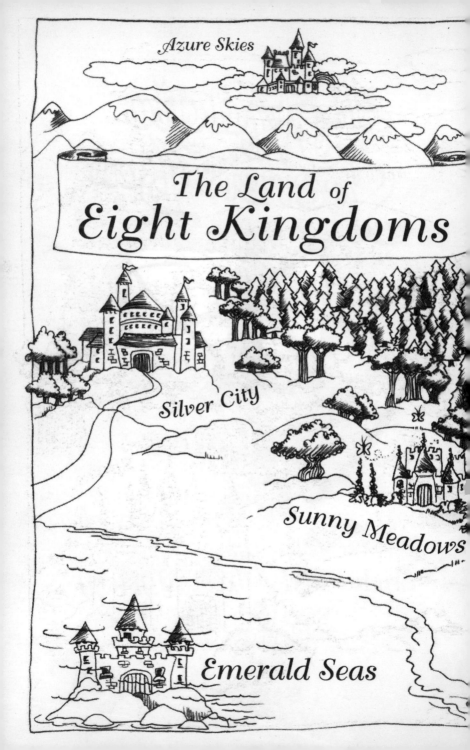

Azure Skies

The Land of
Eight Kingdoms

Silver City

Sunny Meadows

Emerald Seas

The Magic Secrets Box

Chapter One

*S*nuggled under her duvet, Megan Andrews stretched her arms above her head and smiled. It was Saturday morning – hooray! No need to rush out of bed to get ready for school today; no maths lessons, no yucky school dinners… Megan shut her eyes again and rolled over happily. She might as well stay in bed for a bit longer, she thought, yawning.

But just as she was drifting back into a dream, she heard music – sweet, tinkling music, playing in her bedroom. She sat up, suddenly wide awake, her heart racing

with excitement as she recognized the tune – it was coming from her music box! Was the Fairy Queen coming to life again?

She scrambled out of bed, her legs becoming tangled in the duvet in her hurry. She kept her music box on her chest of drawers and as she lifted its brightly-painted lid, she saw that the fairy figure inside was spinning round to the music. A few moments later, the fairy slowed to a halt, then smiled at Megan.

"Good morning," she said.

Megan beamed. "You're back!" she breathed delightedly. Only Megan knew that the pretty box she'd bought from a second-hand shop contained an amazing secret: the Fairy Queen from the Land of Eight Kingdoms was trapped inside! She'd been imprisoned there by a spell

cast by a wicked enchanter, Sorcero, and Megan was on a mission to set her free. Most of the time, the Fairy Queen was a lifeless doll inside the music box, but whenever trouble was brewing in her old home, she was magically brought to life.

Some years earlier, Sorcero had been responsible for looking after the young fairies, elves, mermaids and sprites who lived in the Eight Kingdoms, and he'd used his powerful magic to right any wrongs. He'd been good and kind back then, but when the Fairy Queen had taken over his job, Sorcero's heart had grown cold, and he'd become filled with bitterness. Since he'd imprisoned her, he'd caused chaos in the Silver City with a blundering giant, and struck fear into the Emerald Seas with an enchanted sea monster,

knowing that the Fairy Queen was powerless to help anyone there. Each time, he'd been hoping to sweep in and "save" everyone from danger, and thus become a beloved hero.

Unbeknown to Sorcero, it had been Megan who'd managed to put a stop to his wicked plans. She had also begun to weaken his enchantment on the Fairy Queen. According to the words of his spell, only a true friend to all Eight Kingdoms could free her and so far, Megan had made a friend in both the kingdoms she'd visited. As a result, some parts of the Fairy Queen's body had come back to life – she could move her head and the tips of her fingers on her left hand. But the rest of her was still stiff and unmoving.

"I've got a strong feeling that Sorcero is up to his tricks again," the Fairy Queen said now, looking troubled. "Let's take a look in the magic mirror and find out. If you touch the tip of my wand, I'll use what power I have to make a wish."

Megan leaned over and carefully held the end of the Fairy Queen's tiny wand between her thumb and forefinger. "Ready," she said, feeling excited and nervous all at once.

"Show us Sorcero!" the Fairy Queen commanded.

The wand trembled between Megan's finger and thumb, and a burst of tiny silver sparkles poured from it, flashing and crackling as they streamed round the heart-shaped mirror in the lid of the music box.

The Fairy Queen turned her head, and she and Megan peered into the glass.

As the sparkles faded, an image gradually appeared. It looked like a gloomy, dark cave, and Megan recognized it as Sorcero's spell-chamber. And there was Sorcero himself, leaning back in a chair, his eyes shut and an unpleasant smile twisting his mouth. He wore a dark cloak that dragged on the floor, and he was resting his feet, still shod in muddy boots, up on the table.

A chill ran down Megan's spine. The enchanter was scary even when he was asleep! "He looks very pleased with himself," she said to the Fairy Queen. "I wonder what he's been doing?"

"Look at the leaves on the hem of his cloak," the Fairy Queen replied, narrowing her eyes. "They're from Whispering Willow trees, which only grow in the

Kingdom of the Evergreen Forest. It's a beautiful place, full of woodsprites and woodland animals who live happily and peacefully together. Knowing Sorcero, I fear he may have tried to disturb that peace though."

Megan could see the leaves clinging to the enchanter's cloak. They were long and rather feathery in shape, and bright green with a silvery edging. Then the image in the mirror grew darker and vanished, and she was left looking at her own reflection once more.

The Fairy Queen turned back to Megan. "You have been incredibly brave and helpful so far," she said. "Would you go into the Evergreen Forest for me to see if you can find out what Sorcero has been up to this time?"

A jolt of excitement went through
Megan at the Fairy Queen's words.
Another adventure in the Land of Eight
Kingdoms – how could she refuse? "I'd
love to," she said at once.

The Fairy Queen smiled. "Thank you,"
she said. "And remember to look out for
someone who needs a friend – that seems

to be the way to keep weakening the enchantment Sorcero put on me. Good luck, Megan! While Sorcero sleeps, I hope you will be free from danger, but you must still be careful. And remember, this must remain our secret until I am free."

"I understand," Megan said, her heartbeat quickening.

"Then all you need to do now," the Fairy Queen said, "is touch the end of my wand again and ask to be taken to the Evergreen Forest."

Megan took a deep breath and touched the Fairy Queen's wand. She could feel it pulse between her fingers as if the magic was ready to pour out. "Take me to the Evergreen Forest," she whispered, and in the next second, a stream of silver sparkles flooded out

from the wand, encircling her.

The room seemed to swing around her as Megan felt herself being pulled through the air very fast, with everything blurring before her eyes. She was off on another adventure!

The Magic Secrets Box

Chapter Two

Once Megan's feet had touched solid ground again and the world had stopped spinning, she gazed around in wonder. She was surrounded by tall trees, their leaves swishing mysteriously as a gentle breeze made their branches sway. She recognized the feathery green leaves of a Whispering Willow nearby, whose long branches bent down almost to the ground, the silver edging of the leaves sparkling in the dappled sunlight. There were other trees too, some with twisting branches that went in every direction,

some which stood stiffly upright like
proud soldiers on duty. The leaves of the
trees were vibrant shades of green, red
and gold, and some even had little doors
in the trunks as if tiny creatures lived
there. Megan couldn't stop smiling.
The Evergreen Forest already seemed a
magical place!

Then she remembered to look at her
outfit. When she'd visited Silver City, she'd
been transformed into a ballet dancer, and
down in the Emerald Seas, she'd been a
mermaid with her very own sparkling tail.
This time she was wearing a pretty green
dress, dainty green silk shoes and … Megan
gasped as she realized there was something
strange on her back. She glanced over her
shoulder and laughed as she spotted her
very own pair of shimmering wings,

fluttering slightly in the breeze. "I must be a woodsprite!" she said to herself with delight.

She twitched her shoulder blades experimentally and the next second, her wings lifted her off the ground. Megan gave a squeal of excitement and promptly fell back to earth with a bump.

"Oh my goodness," she whispered under her breath. She could fly! Being a mermaid in the Emerald Seas had been incredible, but being a woodsprite and actually *flying*... Wow. The Land of Eight Kingdoms just got better and better!

The next moment, Megan heard a voice calling through the trees. "Flora! Fenella! Oh, where *are* you?"

She saw a figure fluttering down the woodland path, her golden-edged wings catching the sunlight as she flew. It was another woodsprite. "Flora! Fenella!" she shouted. "Come back!"

When the sprite noticed Megan, she waved and flew over. Her cheeks were pink, her dress was torn, and her hair had leaves and twigs stuck in it as if she'd been scrambling through the undergrowth. She was dressed just like Megan, but with a pine-cone pendant round her neck. "Hello," she said breathlessly, "I don't suppose you've seen two sweet little fawns, have you? They're only babies ... and I've lost them!"

"No, sorry," Megan said. Fawns were baby deer, she remembered. "I ... I haven't been here very long."

The sprite hung her head. "I'm going to be in so much trouble," she confessed with a sigh. "HUGE trouble. I'd just given them their breakfast and was meant to be brushing their coats, but..." Her shoulders drooped. "Well, the thing was, this song popped into my head. It was really good and I was so excited about scribbling down

the tune before I forgot it, that…" She shuffled her feet. "I kind of forgot about the fawns. Only for two minutes! But in that time, they wandered away, and now I've got no idea where they are."

"Oh dear," Megan said sympathetically. She'd seen a fawn once before, when she was staying with her grandma who lived in the countryside. She could still picture its beautiful wide eyes as it had stared at her across the meadow for a long, breathless second. Then it had turned and galloped away with its mother, its cute stumpy tail bobbing as it ran. "Would you like me to help you look for them?" she said, hoping very much that the fawns' disappearance didn't have anything to do with Sorcero. "I'm Megan, by the way."

The sprite looked up eagerly, her green

eyes brightening. "Oh, would you? That would be really kind. I'm Hayley." She tilted her head to one side and frowned as she took a closer look at Megan. "Megan, you say? Have we met before? I don't recognize you."

"No, we haven't met," Megan said carefully. She knew she couldn't tell Hayley the absolute truth about what she was doing in the Evergreen Forest – the last thing she wanted was for word to get back to Sorcero that she was ruining his plans and helping the Fairy Queen! "I'm not from around here," she added, hoping that would be enough of an explanation. "Where should we start looking?"

"Well, I was wondering about using some magic to track them down," Hayley said, "but I can't quite remember the words

of the spell. I'm sooo forgetful. Oh!" She turned to Megan hopefully. "Do *you* know the tracking spell?"

Megan shook her head. She didn't know *any* spells! "Um… No, sorry," she said, feeling awkward. "Why don't you try anyway?" she added encouragingly. "You might remember the whole thing if you start off. My teacher always says—" Then she stopped abruptly, her cheeks turning crimson. Whoops. What was she doing? If she started talking about her teacher, Mrs Harvey, she'd totally give herself away!

Hayley looked confused. "Your teacher?" she repeated. "Do you go to sprite school, then?"

Megan shook her head, tongue-tied. "My teacher… Well, she's actually more of a family friend," she said, crossing her fingers behind her back at the fib. Mrs Harvey was definitely not Megan's friend after all the homework she'd set her recently.

Hayley raised her eyebrows, still seeming puzzled, so Megan quickly asked, "How does the tracking spell start?"

"Hmmm…" Hayley scratched her head. "I *think* I can remember it," she muttered, then haltingly chanted some magical-sounding words. "*Animos* … er … *Fungulus!*" The air shimmered with a strange golden light, and Megan felt her

skin prickle with excitement, eager to see some woodsprite magic in action.

But then Hayley groaned and pointed at the ground. "Oh no. Look!"

Megan gasped as a clump of toadstools nearby suddenly sprouted legs and began marching towards them, their domed caps glimmering with magic. "What's happening?" she asked, staring at the walking toadstools. They looked so sweet and comical!

"Wrong spell," Hayley sighed. "*Arrestium!*" she commanded, pointing at the toadstools. Their legs disappeared and they planted themselves smoothly back into the ground.

Megan wanted to giggle at the peculiar sight she'd just seen, but Hayley was looking so crestfallen, she patted her arm comfortingly instead. "Never mind," said Megan. "Who needs magic? We can just search for the fawns ourselves."

Hayley gave her a grateful smile. "Thanks, Megan," she said. "Let's start looking, then. Follow me."

She fluttered off the ground and Megan immediately flapped her wings too and flew up alongside her, loving the feeling of being in the air. Flying was the most exciting thing ever!

The Magic Secrets Box

Chapter Three

"We'll go to Crystal Falls first," Hayley decided. "The fawns like drinking from the pool at the bottom of the waterfall – they might have gone there."

"Is it your job to look after the fawns?" Megan asked, as a cloud of colourful butterflies flew above their heads. She gave a start as she realized they were all talking to one another in high-pitched tinkling voices.

Hayley nodded. "I help look after the baby animals," she said. "Some of them are orphans, and need feeding and cuddling.

Others need babysitting while their parents are out finding food." She grinned. "And all of them love my lullabies at night-time. It's my favourite bit of the whole day, seeing their eyes slowly closing as they're curled up in their cosy beds. It's the cutest thing ever!"

"Oh, I wish I could see that!" Megan smiled.

"I'll show you later," Hayley promised. "If we find the fawns, and I haven't been banished from the kingdom, that is." She smiled weakly, but Megan could tell she was worried.

They both flew on, calling for the fawns at intervals and scouring the woodland for a sign of the missing animals. They saw foxes, woodpeckers, a sweet family of fluffy rabbits, and even

a spiky hedgehog, his beady eyes black and bright, all of whom greeted the sprites in a friendly fashion. Hayley kept swooping down to ask the animals if they'd noticed the two young fawns go by, but not a single creature had seen them.

"We're nearly at Crystal Falls," Hayley said after a while, still pale and anxious. "I just hope they're there. They don't seem to be anywhere else."

Megan was starting to feel worried about the fawns too. She couldn't help remembering that unpleasant smirk on Sorcero's face she'd seen in the magic mirror. Had he done something to them?

"We'll find them," she assured her new friend, although the words rang hollow even to her own ears. "Let's keep searching. They can't have gone too far."

Just then a fox limped out from behind
a tree, looking rather sorry for himself.
His pointed ears were flattened, his
whiskers drooped and his thick coppery
tail dragged along the ground behind him.

"Are you all right?" Hayley asked in
concern. She flew down to the ground
and hurried over to him. Megan quickly
followed.

"I've hurt my leg," the fox said, holding
his paw gingerly in the air. His whiskers
trembled with pain. "Any chance you
could use some magic to make it better?"

"Of course," Hayley said at once, giving
him a gentle stroke. "Um… Let me see."
She screwed up her face, then nodded to
herself. "I *think* I can remember the words
of the healing spell," she murmured to
Megan. "I'll try it anyway."

She pointed a finger at the fox.
"*Vulpus ... portis ... wool!*" she declared.
The air around them sparkled with a
million golden lights, and then Hayley
and Megan both gasped in surprise. Long,
green woolly socks had appeared on the
fox's four legs!

Hayley clapped a hand to her mouth and turned red. "Oops," she said, looking embarrassed. "Sorry about that. Wrong spell. Obviously."

"They're very cosy," the fox said kindly. "But perhaps you could try again?"

"Sure," Hayley said. "Um…"

"Take your time," Megan urged, seeing that her new friend was starting to look flustered.

Hayley nodded, a little frown creasing her forehead as she thought. "OK," she said after a minute. "*Vulpus … portis … WELL!*"

There came another flurry of golden sparkles, this time looping round and round the fox's injured leg just like a magical bandage, Megan thought, her eyes wide. The green socks vanished along

with the sparkles, and the fox gave his leg
a careful shake. He put his paw down and
tested his weight on it – then smiled.
"You did it! Well done," he cheered, and
rushed round in a circle, his tail beating
happily from side to side. "Thank you
so much."

Hayley beamed with pride. "You're
very welcome," she said, as the fox ran
to her and pressed his head gratefully
against her side. She stroked his thick
coat and Megan couldn't resist reaching
over and doing the same. What would
her best friends at school say if she told
them she'd actually stroked a real fox?
A talking fox, no less! Nobody would
ever believe her.

"Now that you're feeling better,
perhaps you could help me," Hayley went

on to the fox. "I don't suppose you've seen a pair of gorgeous fawns, have you? About this tall, big brown eyes and long eyelashes, spotty coats…?"

The fox nodded, his sharp eyes bright. "Yes, I've seen them," he replied. "They were heading for Crystal Falls."

"Hooray!" Hayley cheered, flinging her arms around the fox's neck. "I was hoping they'd be there. Oh, you clever fox, I'm so glad we met you."

"Brilliant!" Megan said happily. "That's really good news."

The fox stared at them. "Good news?" he repeated in surprise. "Hardly. Haven't you heard about the ogre?"

Megan started at the fox's words. An *ogre*? She didn't like the sound of that. She'd read about ogres in fairytales and

they were always unfriendly, brutish creatures.

"Gripnorth? The ogre who lives in the cave behind the waterfall? Oh, he's a big softy," Hayley scoffed.

"Not any more," the fox said, looking serious. "I don't know what's happened to him, but he's in a fearsome mood today. If the fawns have wandered into his cave, I'm afraid they're in terrible danger!"

Chapter Four

Megan gulped. "What's happened? Why is he in such a bad mood?" she asked. The Evergreen Forest had seemed such a friendly place – until now.

"That's the strange thing," the fox replied. "Nobody really knows. Normally he doesn't mind the woodland animals walking through his cave to get to the drinking pool. But apparently he's not letting any of them through today. In fact, he's trapped them in his cave!"

Hayley stared. "You mean, he's keeping them prisoner?"

The fox nodded. "Be careful, won't you?" he said. "I'm staying well away." He loped off into the woods, his russet tail swinging behind him.

Megan turned to Hayley. "What do you think we should do?" she asked.

"We're going to see for ourselves what Gripnorth's doing, that's what," Hayley said, with a determined jut of her chin. "And if he's dared take my fawns prisoner, then we're going to rescue them!"

Megan had had a feeling that Hayley was going to say that. "O-OK," she replied as bravely as she could. After all, she was here to put things right and to help a new friend – and right now, Hayley definitely needed her help.

The two woodsprites took to the air once more and flew towards the waterfall.

The fact that a usually nice ogre had turned aggressive made Megan feel suspicious. She was sure this must have something to do with Sorcero! In Silver City, he'd enchanted a giant to keep dancing through the streets, knowing that his enormous thumping feet would bring the buildings crashing down. And in the Emerald Seas, he'd sent a sea monster to terrify the mermaids. Megan's heart beat faster at the thought of having to deal with an angry ogre this time. She hoped he wouldn't decide to keep her and Hayley prisoner too!

Moments later, Megan and Hayley arrived at the top of Crystal Falls: a magnificent glassy sheet of water tumbling over shiny black rocks, all the way down to a deep, clear pool below.

"The cave is through there," Hayley whispered, pointing to a dark opening in the rocks to one side of the waterfall. They could hear an angry roaring sound from within, and Hayley clutched Megan's hand and held it tightly. "Thank you for coming with me, Megan," she added. "I'd be even more scared without you."

Megan squeezed Hayley's hand. "Let's creep inside and see what's happening," she whispered back.

Cautiously, the two sprites clambered through the opening in the rocks. Megan blinked a few times as her eyes grew used to the darkness, then she saw that they were in a sort of tunnel. Water dripped from the ceiling, making the rocky ground slippery. The two friends tiptoed carefully along the passageway.

After they'd gone only a short way, the passage opened out into a large, gloomy cave, and Hayley and Megan hovered in the shadows, gazing nervously around. Overhead came the sound of rushing water from the falls, and Megan could see, diagonally across from them, the exit to the cave – the way that the animals

would usually take to get to the drinking pool. Today, however, the path was barred with a pile of rocks, which blocked out most of the light. A fire had been lit in the centre of the cave, and the flames crackled, sending up orange sparks and billowing woodsmoke into the darkness.

Hayley nudged Megan and pointed to the back corner of the cave. Through the smoky gloom, Megan could just make out the faces of two terrified little fawns as well as a number of rabbits, a badger and three squirrels huddled together. But worse than the sight of all those frightened animals was seeing the ogre himself. He was a huge, lumpy creature with a misshapen head, cruel piggy eyes and hands like shovels.

A chill went down Megan's spine as she watched him balance a gigantic cooking pot on the fire and grunt nastily to himself. He was clearly planning to cook the woodland creatures in a stew!

Hayley gave a sharp intake of breath as she realized the same thing – and then before Megan could stop her, the brave woodsprite strode right out into the middle of the cave. "Stop, Gripnorth!" she called indignantly. "What are you *doing*? These animals haven't done you any harm! Let them go free at once!"

Despite her absolute terror at the look on the ogre's face as he swung round towards Hayley, Megan couldn't leave her friend alone to face his fury. She sidled out of the shadows and stood next to her, heart pounding. "P-p-please let us take them back into the woods where they belong," she stammered.

Megan trembled from head to foot as the ogre gave a roar of anger that seemed to shake the ground beneath their feet.

"Let them go free? Ha!" he thundered. "You silly sprites. I can't just let them go!"

"We couldn't answer the riddle, Hayley," one of the fawns said timidly, hanging her pretty head.

"And now he's going to eat us!" the other one whimpered.

"What riddle? What do you mean?" Hayley asked.

"SILENCE!" bellowed the ogre, picking up a rock and hurling it against the cave wall. It smashed into pieces and one of the rabbits hid its head in its paws. "Stop talking, you wretched creatures. I haven't had a minute's peace – how's an ogre meant to think straight with all this *noise*?" He glared around and a deathly silence fell over the cave. Megan held her breath, terrified.

"Gripnorth, I don't understand," Hayley said tentatively. "This isn't like you. Usually you're friends with the animals of the Evergreen Forest. I didn't think you minded them coming through your cave."

Hayley's soft voice seemed to take the anger out of the ogre. He kicked sullenly at another stone, his shoulders drooping. "I just want to go to sleep," he muttered. "I'm so tired. All I want to do is sleep."

Megan exchanged a look with Hayley. "What if we could help you get to sleep?" she asked. "Hayley sings the baby animals of the forest to sleep with her wonderful lullabies. If she were to sing for you, I'm sure you would doze off in no time."

"Yes!" Hayley said eagerly. "Of course! Lie down, dear Gripnorth, and let me sing you to sleep."

But instead of looking pleased by their suggestion, the ogre's temper seemed worse than ever. He lunged towards the two woodsprites, his eyes blazing. "I CAN'T!" he bellowed. "Don't you understand? I can't sleep!"

Hayley and Megan shrank back in terror. Megan's legs were like jelly as she felt the ogre's hot, stinking breath on her face.

"I've got to guard the drinking pool, haven't I?" the ogre went on. "Night and day! And that's making me very HUNGRY and BAD-TEMPERED. Now beat it … unless you want to end up in my cooking pot too?"

Megan glanced at Hayley, then back at Gripnorth. The fox hadn't said anything about the ogre having to guard the drinking pool. "What do you mean, guard the pool?" she asked, feeling very small and very scared.

"I mean what I say, you silly little sprite," he shouted. "I've been put in charge of the pool round the clock. I can't let anyone through until someone's answered the riddle correctly. And the man said that if anyone got it wrong, I was allowed to COOK them!" He waved an arm at the

shivering, frightened creatures in the corner. "Guess what?" he snarled, showing his huge yellow teeth. "They ALL got it wrong. So I may be tired, but at least I'm going to have a feast tonight."

Megan's stomach had lurched inside her when the ogre mentioned "the man". That *had* to be Sorcero!

"The man?" Hayley repeated, frowning. "What man?"

The ogre looked as if he was becoming impatient with their questions. "The man with the cloak and the wand," he growled. "So. Are you two going to try your luck with the riddle – or have you suddenly changed your minds about your little animal rescue?" He licked his lips.

Hayley was still looking utterly confused by this conversation so Megan,

seeing the ogre was on the verge of losing his temper, quickly pulled her friend back into the passageway.

"I don't understand," Hayley whispered, looking upset. "The man with a cloak and a wand – who could that be? And what's this riddle?"

"It must be some kind of horrible enchanter or wizard," Megan replied carefully, not wanting to give away just how much she knew. "And it looks like he's put a spell on the ogre that can only be broken when someone works out the answer to the riddle."

Inside she was seething. By enchanting the ogre, Sorcero was effectively cutting off the animals' water supply, which could be disastrous! And if none of them knew the answer, then even more animals

would end up trapped in this horrible
cave, and maybe even cooked in a stew!

They had to get the poor animals out
of there, and somehow break the spell.
But how?

The Magic Secrets Box

Chapter Five

"What are we going to *do?*" Hayley whispered, her eyes filling with tears. "This is awful! We can't just leave the animals there, but he's so angry I'm scared he's going to stuff *us* in the pot too. And where's the Fairy Queen?" she added desperately. "Normally, she'd have sorted this out with her magic. Why hasn't she come to help us?"

"Maybe she … can't get here right now," Megan said uneasily. Well, it was true, she thought, picturing the poor Fairy Queen trapped in the music box back at home.

"As for this enchanter ... I don't know what to think!" Hayley went on, not seeming to notice Megan's awkwardness. "Where has he come from? I don't know whether we should rush to the palace to tell the King and Queen about it, or—"

"I think we need to stop the ogre making his stew first," Megan pointed out. "Let's get the animals to safety, and then we can worry about the enchanter. We need to find out what this riddle is, and work it out."

"But if we *can't* work it out…" Hayley said helplessly. Neither sprite spoke for a moment. It did seem a terrible gamble, asking the ogre for a riddle they might not be able to solve. "Maybe we should try something else first," she went on, then brightened. "What if I could distract

Gripnorth somehow? I could dazzle him with some magic while you nip into the cave and set the animals free…"

Megan hesitated. Much as she liked her friend and wanted to help free the trapped animals, she wasn't sure that this was the best idea. What if the spell went wrong, and that tipped the ogre into an even fouler temper?

A better idea came to her in the next moment. "Maybe … maybe we could offer Gripnorth something else really tasty to eat instead of his stew," she said slowly. "That way he might let the animals go free, and it'll give us some time to work out the riddle."

"Good thinking," Hayley said, nodding. She glanced around the rocky passage. "Um … I wonder if he likes toadstools?"

she said, seeing a couple growing there.

Megan shook her head. "You've seen
how big he is," she said. "And he's starving
hungry. A few toadstools won't fill him
up. No, we need something really big and
tasty to tempt him. Could you use your
magic to conjure up a lovely vegetable
stew for him? Or a delicious pie?"

"Um…" Hayley said doubtfully. "I could
give it a go…"

Megan's confidence began to ebb away
as she imagined Hayley's magic going
wrong again. Perhaps it hadn't been such
a good idea after all. She was just trying to
think of something else, when she heard
one of the fawns give a nervous squeak.
The sound seemed to spur Hayley into
action.

"Well, I'm going to have to try," she said,

a determined expression on her face.
"I'm not sure I've got the spell completely
right, but what else can we do?"

Megan nodded. Time was running out.
They had to act quickly!

She and Hayley crept back to the cave.
The ogre was now dropping herbs into the
boiling water as it churned inside his
cooking pot. "Now," he muttered gleefully,
clapping his hands together and eyeing the
terrified animals, "who's going in first?"

"Wait!" yelled Megan, as she and
Hayley rushed forward.

"Not you two again," the ogre growled.

"We've had an idea," Hayley gabbled.
"We want to make you an offer, Gripnorth.
To save you all the work of cooking these
animals – which, let's face it, is going to
take HOURS – how about we give you a
delicious hot dinner right now instead?"

"You said you were really hungry,"
Megan put in coaxingly. "So how about it?
You let the animals go, and we'll give you
a yummy replacement meal. You could be
tucking in in just two minutes!"

The ogre's tummy gave a loud gurgle.
"Hmmm," he said. Then he shook his
head, a crafty glint in his eye. "Ahh, but
rules are rules. These animals didn't know
the riddle. They can't go even if I let them.

The magic has held them here."

Megan thought quickly. She could see he was tempted. "OK, well how about this," she suggested bravely. "If we make you a lovely hot dinner now, at least you'll have a nice full tummy again very soon. And you can save these animals for the next time you feel hungry." Anything to give them more thinking time was a bonus, she reckoned.

The ogre narrowed his eyes and thought for a moment. There was silence in the cave, save for the rushing waterfall outside and the crackling fire. At long last, he nodded. "All right," he said. "We have a deal. I quite fancy a pie, now that you mention it."

"Brilliant," Megan said in relief. "One delicious hot pie coming right up!"

Hayley cleared her throat. She looked petrified.

"Take your time," Megan reminded her, trying to smile encouragingly at her friend.

There was another terrible silence. All the animals seemed to be holding their breath as Hayley raised a shaking finger and began to chant some magical words. "*Culinarum ... yummina ... plattorio!*"

There was a puff of smoke, and a flash of golden light. And then the smoke cleared, and everyone stared.

Megan felt faint with dismay. Instead of conjuring up a steaming pie, Hayley had magicked up a massive chocolate cake with elaborate swirls of icing.

"Oh no," Hayley groaned weakly. "Wrong spell. AGAIN!"

Chapter Six

"What's *that*?" Gripnorth roared.
"Because it doesn't look like a
delicious hot pie to *me*!"

The colour had drained from Hayley's
face. "I'm so sorry," she whispered, edging
away. "I must have got muddled up."

Megan could hardly bear to look. The
ogre's face was purple with fury as he
picked up a rock and hurled it at the cake.

SPLAT! Chocolate icing sprayed all over
the ogre: it landed in his hair, across his
face and over his clothes. There was even
a big blob right on the end of his nose.

At any other time, it might have been very funny. At this precise moment though, Megan had never felt so sick with fright. With an almighty roar, Gripnorth rushed towards Hayley and Megan, shaking his fist.

Hayley screamed and clutched at Megan. "No!" she cried fearfully.

But then, just as Megan was expecting the worst, something wonderful happened. The blob of icing plopped off the ogre's noise … and fell straight into his wide-open roaring mouth.

Gripnorth stopped immediately. His eyes widened as he tasted the chocolate. And then, to Megan's complete and utter surprise, he smiled. "Mmmm," he said. "Tastes good."

Hayley had her hands over her eyes

and Megan elbowed her. "Look," she hissed excitedly.

The ogre sat down in front of the cake and plunged a hand into it, breaking off a large chunk. He crammed this into his mouth and chewed, shutting his eyes in blissful delight. "Better than pie!" he declared with his mouth full, spraying crumbs everywhere. "Better than stew. It's DELICIOUS!"

Hayley and Megan grinned at one another. "Maybe it wasn't the wrong spell after all," Megan said, squeezing her friend's hand proudly. "Maybe it was the *perfect* spell!"

"And the animals are safe for a little while longer, at least," Hayley said shakily. "Thank goodness for that."

Just then, a glorious white unicorn trotted into the cave. He had a mane that sparkled golden, even in the gloomy cave, and his coat was pure white. He whickered uncertainly when he saw the ogre, the sprites and the trapped animals all crowding the cave. "Greetings, Gripnorth," he sniffed haughtily. "May I pass to drink at the pool?"

Gripnorth, who now had chocolate smeared all round his mouth, smirked.

"You may if you can solve my riddle, Dobbin," he said craftily, then cleared his throat, as if he were about to recite it.

"Wait!" Megan said quickly to the unicorn. "It's a trap!"

The unicorn stamped a golden hoof impatiently and tossed his mane. "Do not worry, sprite," he said. "I am sure I can answer a simple riddle. Carry on, Gripnorth. I am ready."

Hayley opened her mouth to protest, but the ogre was too quick for her. She and Megan could only listen in horror as he spoke the words of the riddle.

"Give me food and I will live. Give me water and I will die. What am I?"

The unicorn tossed his gleaming mane. "Simple," he said. "It's quite simple. The answer is, of course…" Then he hesitated, his nostrils flaring. "I don't know," he admitted.

The ogre smirked. "Oh dear," he gloated. "And by the way, I forgot to tell you the most important part. If you don't

answer the riddle correctly, you're going
in my cooking pot, along with all these
other animals. Ha ha!"

The unicorn stamped his hoof again.
"You can't do that," he retorted. "I forbid
you, you stinking ogre. Don't you dare lay
a finger on me!"

"I don't need to," Gripnorth said lazily,
grabbing another chunk of cake and
shoving it into his mouth.

"Well, I refuse to take part in this
ridiculous game," the unicorn said. "I'll
just find somewhere else to drink."

But as he tried to turn and gallop out
of the cave, a plume of purple and black
smoke appeared, wreathing round his
hooves. Megan and Hayley watched in
alarm as the unicorn's legs walked
themselves over to the other animals at

the back of the cave, even though the unicorn clearly didn't want to go there.

"How are you doing this?" he cried furiously. "Stop it at once! There's still time for me to answer the riddle, you know!"

The ogre merely laughed. "That's what they all say," he sneered. "Keep thinking, Dobbin."

Megan was thinking too. Her mind was racing, trying to figure out the ogre's riddle. "Give me water and I will die," he'd said. Could it be some kind of plant or animal that didn't like water? Maybe something living in a desert?

She pulled Hayley back into the tunnel so that they could talk. "We've got to work out this riddle before any more animals come along and become trapped," she whispered. "Any ideas?"

"Not a thing," Hayley replied glumly. "I'm starting to feel scared, Megan. I was hoping the cake might sweeten him up, but he seems more horrible than ever. Think! What could the answer be?"

The Magic Secrets Box

Chapter Seven

"'**G**ive me food and I will live...'"
Megan said thoughtfully. "'Give me water and I will die.' Hmmm. How would water make anything die? Everything needs water to live, doesn't it?"

"Perhaps it's something to do with drowning?" Hayley said, wrinkling her nose. "Or maybe the answer is some kind of insect that doesn't like water. Butterflies and bees don't like getting their wings wet, do they?"

"True," Megan said. "But—"

"Let's try that," Hayley said, and was all

set to march back into the cave when Megan grabbed hold of her.

"Hold on," she said. "We've got to be absolutely sure about this. You saw what he was like with the unicorn. If we can't answer the riddle correctly, we're going to get that horrible smoke round *our* feet too, and the next thing you know, we'll end up in the stew."

She shuddered as she pictured the cooking pot still steaming away on the fire. And then a smile broke out on her face and she let out a cry of delight as the answer tumbled right into her head. "That's it!" she gabbled excitedly. "That's the answer – *fire*! Water puts out fire, doesn't it? I think the answer to the riddle must be fire!"

"'Give me food and I will live…'" Hayley

said, and nodded. "Yes – you can feed a fire with wood or fuel. And 'give me water and I will die' – yes again. Giving a fire water will put it out. I think you're right!"

Hayley was beaming, her eyes bright, but Megan still felt tense. The answer to the riddle *seemed* right – but there might be more than one correct answer. "Well, there's only one way to find out," Megan said. "Come on, let's give it a try."

The two woodsprites went back into the cave. "We would like to try and solve your riddle," Hayley announced, casting a nervous sideways smile at the fawns.

The ogre, who had just eaten another enormous mouthful of chocolate cake, let out a satisfied burp. "Oho! Think you're clever enough, do you?" he taunted.

Megan's heart hammered. "I hope so,"

she mumbled. She could feel the eyes of all the animals on her and felt horribly responsible for them. If her answer turned out to be wrong…

"Then let me ask you the riddle and we shall see," the ogre said. "Give me food and I will live. Give me water and I will die. WHAT AM I?"

He roared the last words at top volume and they echoed around the cave.

Megan took a deep breath. "You are … FIRE!"

As she cried out the word, there was a blinding flash of light, and purple sparks flew all around the ogre.

Thick black smoke filled the cave, and Megan dimly heard Hayley and the animals coughing and spluttering. She fanned away the smoke, her heart thumping, unsure as to what had just happened. Was her guess right – or was she about to become the next ingredient in the ogre's cooking pot?

The smoke finally cleared to reveal that the boulders blocking the cave exit had vanished. The ogre, meanwhile, was blinking and looking confused. "I'm so tired," he murmured, his eyes closing. He jerked them open again and stared at Megan and Hayley. Then he smiled. "I think you did it," he said. "I think you broke the enchantment. I think ... ZZZZ."

The next second, he had keeled over sideways, narrowly missing the remains of

the cake, and began snoring contentedly.
Hayley flung her arms round Megan.
"You did it!" she squealed. "Oh, Megan,
well done. That was amazing!"

Megan beamed. "*We* did it, you mean,"
she said joyfully. "Your amazing chocolate
cake stopped him from eating the animals,
there and then, don't forget. And now
they're all free again!"

Flora and Fenella trotted over to Megan and Hayley and pushed their noses gratefully into the woodsprites' hands. "Thank you for rescuing us," they said in sweet, high-pitched voices. "We're sorry we wandered off this morning, Hayley. We promise we won't do it again."

"That's all right," Hayley said, kissing them each in turn. "Let's go home. Oh, but first…"

She darted out of the cave into the woods, and Megan smiled to hear her shout: "EVERYONE! The riddle has been solved. The ogre's asleep. It's safe to come and drink from the pool again!"

The Magic Secrets Box

Chapter Eight

*T*he other animals crowded round Megan and Hayley, thanking them for their bravery. The unicorn bowed low in front of them. "I should have listened to you when you tried to warn me about the riddle," he said apologetically. "Thank you for saving our lives. You will be lifelong friends of unicorns everywhere from this day forward."

Megan stroked his velvety nose, admiring the gleam of his twisted horn. "That's all right," she told him, thrilled to be a friend of one unicorn, let alone

all of them. "I'm really glad we could help."

Once the animals had had a lovely long drink at the pool, Megan and Hayley took the fawns home.

"This is the woodland nursery," Hayley said, leading Megan, Flora and Fenella to a large log cabin with separate sections for each sort of animal. A group of bright-eyed baby bunnies had just enjoyed a hopping lesson with their proud mum, and were being taken back to their burrow, and three russet fox cubs were tumbling playfully round another pen.

"It's lovely here," Megan sighed happily, breathing in the sweet scent from the pretty star-shaped white flowers that bloomed nearby.

Hayley grinned. "It's good to be back."

It was growing dark, so after giving the

fawns some juicy leaves to nibble, Megan and Hayley tucked Flora and Fenella into their cosy straw beds. Then Hayley sang all the baby animals a lullaby until their heads drooped and their eyes closed.

Hayley was right, Megan thought, smiling at the snoozing animals – it really was the sweetest thing she'd ever seen!

Just then, a dark-haired woodsprite popped her head round the door. "Hayley! What *have* you been doing? The King and Queen have summoned you to the palace," she said anxiously.

Hayley gulped. "Oh dear!" she said, looking flustered. "They must have heard about the ogre. I hope I'm not in trouble."

Megan was just about to offer to accompany her friend when she heard the tinkling melody from her music box, and knew her adventure in the Evergreen Forest was almost over. "Oh, no," she cried in dismay. "I've got to go home now. I wish I could stay longer with you."

"You're going? Where to?" Hayley asked. "When will I see you again?"

Megan bit her lip. "I don't know," she replied truthfully. "I'm not from this kingdom." She shrugged. "I can't explain. But I've so enjoyed meeting you, Hayley. I'll never forget you."

Hayley hugged her again. "Me neither," she said. "Thanks for everything. You're the

best friend I've ever had. Here." She took
the pine-cone necklace from round her
neck and pressed it into Megan's hand.
"Have this to remember me by."

The music was getting louder, and the
Kingdom of Evergreen Forest began to
blur before Megan's eyes. "Thank you,
Hayley!" she called, hurrying out of sight
as she felt the magic pulling at her.
"Goodbye!"

And then she was swept up and the kingdom was completely gone. Bright lights flashed around her and she was hurtling through the air, faster and faster…

Moments later, she felt soft carpet beneath her bare feet and opened her eyes to see that she was back in her bedroom. It was still Saturday morning, and according to her clock, no time had passed. The pine-cone pendant was now in her music box, gleaming with magic.

"Wow," she said, smiling at the Fairy Queen. "That was exciting."

The Fairy Queen suddenly gasped. "I can move the whole of my left arm now!" she realized joyfully, lifting it up and down in excitement. "You must have made another friend!" She beamed.

"Once again, the power of friendship has weakened Sorcero's enchantment. Well done, Megan. Tell me all about it."

Megan sat on her bed and told the Fairy Queen everything that had happened, the tinkling music still playing softly in the background. The Fairy Queen looked appalled as she heard how Sorcero had put so many animals' lives at risk. "That's awful," she cried. "Oh, I can't bear being trapped here and being so useless. Thank goodness you were able to solve the riddle and set them free."

Megan smiled. "Hayley and I were a good team," she said. "I couldn't have

done it without her." She gazed into the distance. "I hope she'll be all right," she went on. "When I left, she'd just been summoned to see the King and Queen."

"The King and Queen of the Evergreen Forest are wise and fair," the Fairy Queen replied. "I'm sure they will reward Hayley's bravery."

Just then, Megan noticed that the tinkling music had slowed down, and she felt a pang of dismay. Oh no! She knew that once the music stopped, the Fairy Queen would go back to being a tiny doll that couldn't move or speak. "I hope I'll see you again before long," she said hurriedly. "Thanks for—"

But to Megan's disappointment, the music had already stopped, and in the next second, the Fairy Queen had lost the

bright sparkle in her eyes. The pine-cone pendant no longer twinkled with magic, but rather looked like an ordinary one. Megan's shoulders drooped as her bedroom returned to its quiet, ordinary self. The adventure was over.

She gently touched the Fairy Queen's plastic crown, wishing the magic hadn't ended so quickly. "I'm here whenever you need me," she whispered. "And I'll do everything I can to set you free."

Then she bobbed a little curtsey and skipped downstairs, still in her pyjamas. She was starving after all her adventures! "Can we do some baking later today, Mum?" she asked, as she sat at the kitchen table and began tucking into her breakfast.

"Of course," her mum said. "What shall we make?"

Megan grinned. "How about a chocolate cake?" she suggested. "Let's make a cake big enough to feed a hungry ogre!"

Her mum laughed. "You and your imagination," she said. "I don't know where you come up with these crazy ideas."

Megan smiled to herself. She knew *exactly* what had given her the idea – but she wasn't about to tell her mum. Some things were definitely best kept a secret!

Epilogue

All was peaceful at Crystal Falls when Sorcero reappeared there in a swirl of black and purple smoke later that day. He made his way towards the tunnel with a wicked smile on his face, listening out for the ogre's roars and the squeals of fright from the animals he'd captured. Oh, it was going to be wonderful. What a hero he would be, sweeping in to rescue them all!

But as he approached the rocky tunnel that led to the cave, his confidence gave way to confusion. All he could hear was a rumbling sound. What on earth was *that*?

He rounded the corner into the cave and stared in shocked fury at the sight of Gripnorth the ogre fast asleep on his back,

snoring like a baby. Asleep? The fearsome ogre was actually *asleep*?

Had someone really solved the riddle and broken the enchantment already? It appeared so. Of all the bad luck!

Scowling furiously, Sorcero pulled his cloak round himself and stormed out of the cave. Next time, he vowed, he'd cast an even more fiendish enchantment. And next time, he wouldn't fall asleep himself and miss out on all the action, either.

"I'll be watching," he snarled under his breath, glaring around the peaceful woodland scene. "And *nothing* will go wrong!"